THIS WALKER BOOK BELONGS TO:

D0318378

First published 1993 by Walker Books Ltd
87 Vauxhall Walk, London SE11 5HJ

This edition published 1998

2 4 6 8 10 9 7 5 3

Printed in Hong Kong

British Library Cataloguing in Publication Data
A catalogue record for this book is
available from the British Library.

ISBN 0-7445-6315-1

Who's on the Farm?

Naomi Russell

WALKER BOOKS
AND SUBSIDIARIES
LONDON • BOSTON • SYDNEY

Who's waiting
by the gate?

The dog.

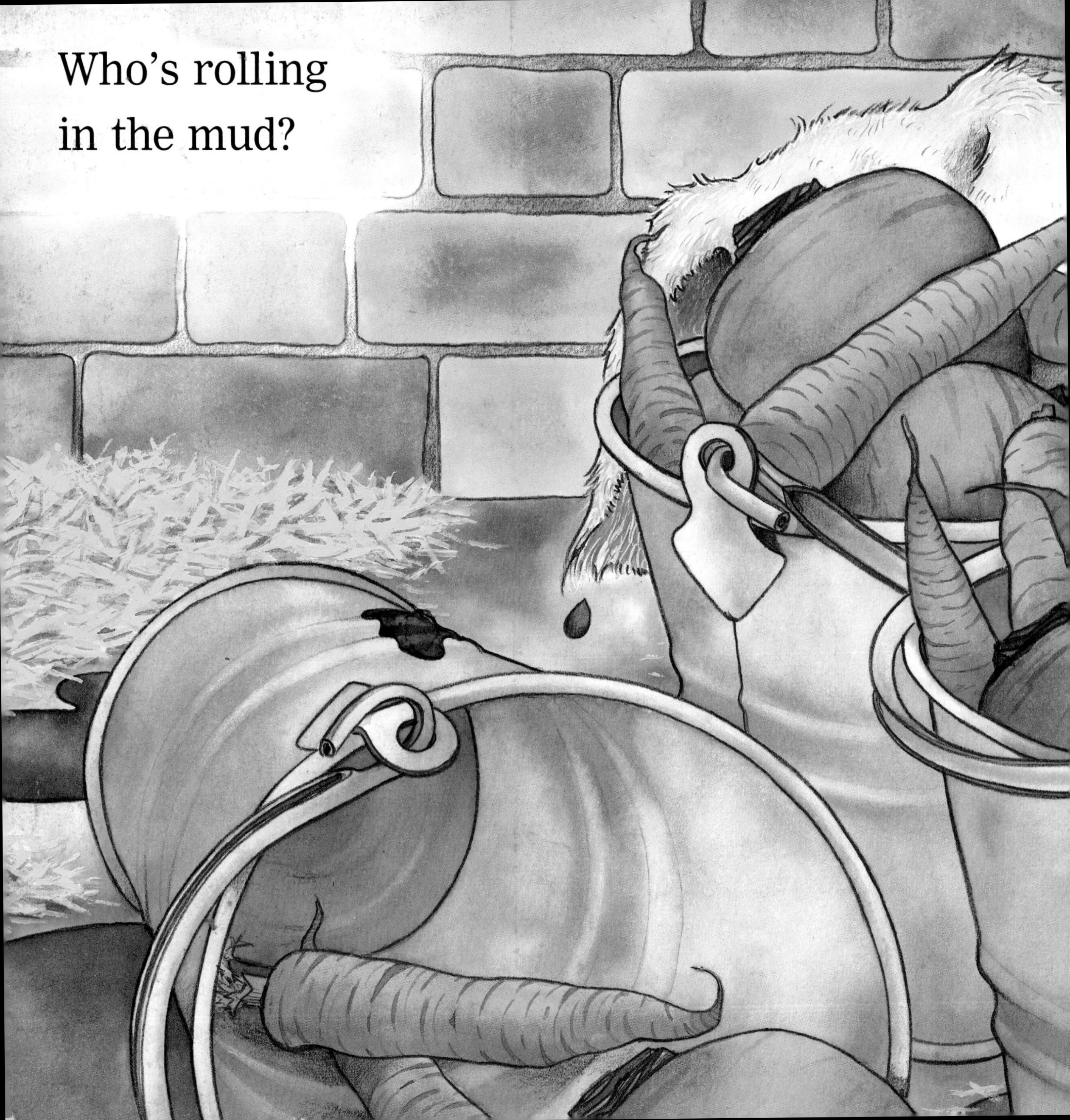

Who's rolling
in the mud?

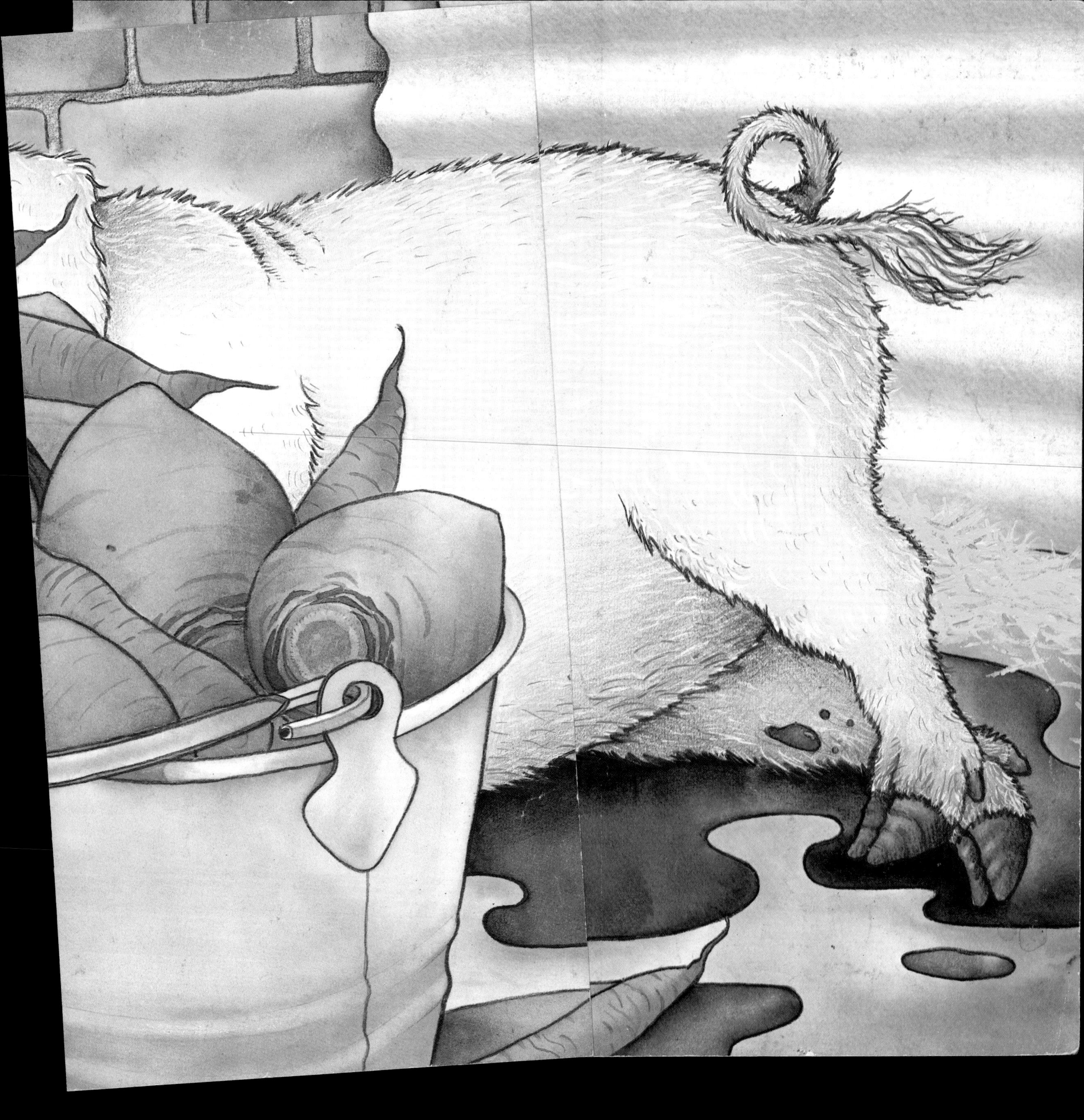

Who's splashing
in the stream?

Who's running in the field?

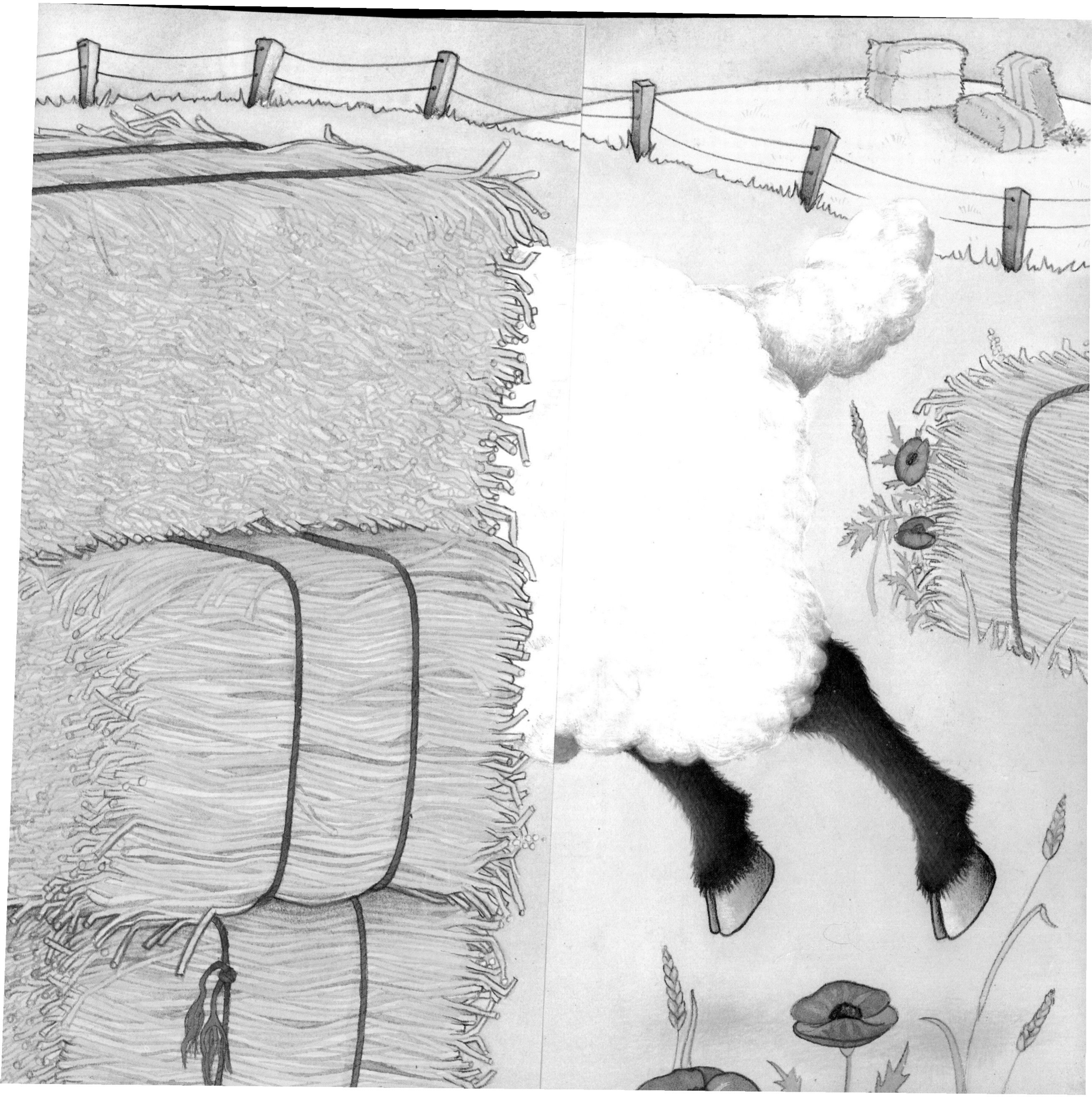

Who's munching grass?

The cow.

And who's
in the basket?
Look...

MORE WALKER PAPERBACKS

For You to Enjoy

TICKLE MONSTER

by Paul Rogers/Jo Burroughes

If you're ticklish, you'd better watch out – the Tickle Monster's about! Where is he? Flip the flaps and see!

0-7445-6310-0 £3.99

WHAT DO I LOOK LIKE?

by Nick Sharratt

How do you look when you're having fun or feeling cross? When you bang your thumb or get an ice-cream? Flip the flaps and see!

0-7445-6311-9 £3.99

WHERE'S MY EGG?

by Tony Mitton/Jane Chapman

Hen has lost her egg. Is it in Ben's kennel or Puss's bed or Donkey's straw? Where can it be? Flip the flaps and see!

0-7445-6312-7 £3.99